a sweet smell *of* roses

by **angela johnson** · *illustrated by* **eric velasquez**

Simon & Schuster Books for Young Readers

New York London Toronto Sydney

To Jessie Chase, who was there in the beginning—A. J.

To my friend Tom Feelings—E. V.

SIMON & SCHUSTER BOOKS FOR YOUNG READERS

An imprint of Simon & Schuster Children's Publishing Division

1230 Avenue of the Americas, New York, New York 10020

Text copyright © 2005 by Angela Johnson

Illustrations copyright © 2005 by Eric Velasquez

All rights reserved, including the right of reproduction in whole or in part in any form.

SIMON & SCHUSTER BOOKS FOR YOUNG READERS is a trademark of Simon & Schuster, Inc.

Book design by Greg Stadnyk

The text for this book is set in Century Schoolbook.

The illustrations for this book are rendered in charcoal.

Manufactured in the United States of America

10 9 8 7 6 5 4 3 2 1

CIP data for this book is available from the Library of Congress.

ISBN 0-689-83252-4

about the book

When we learn about the Civil Rights movement that blew across the American landscape in the 1950s and 1960s, certain names always arise. Thurgood Marshall. Rosa Parks. Ralph Abernathy. Fannie Lou Hamer. Medgar Evers. Malcolm X. Robert Kennedy. And of course, Dr. Martin Luther King. These are all important names. Each belongs to a man or woman who sacrificed much—sometimes everything—in the quest for freedom and justice. But the men and women we commonly hear about are not the only ones who took action against injustice and oppression. For each of the names that we know, there are tens of thousands that we do not. And some of those overlooked names belong to children. *A Sweet Smell of Roses* is a tribute to them. The brave boys and girls who—like their adult counterparts—could not resist the scent of freedom carried aloft by the winds of change.

from the artist

The two men who inspired my work in this book, Harvey Dinnerstein and Burton Silverman, are no strangers to the fine-art community. Dinnerstein's work can be found in the collections of the Smithsonian, the Metropolitan Museum of Art, and the Whitney Museum of American Art. Silverman's paintings have graced the covers of *Time, Newsweek,* and *New York* magazines, as well as the collections of the Brooklyn Museum, the Philadelphia Museum of Art, and the National Museum of American Art. But I first became aware of Harvey Dinnerstein and Burt Silverman in high school when my illustration teacher brought in the then newly published books: *Harvey Dinnerstein: Artist at Work* and Burt Silverman's *Painting People*. Both books recounted how these men had gone to Alabama in 1956 during the Montgomery Bus Boycott and documented the events in a series of drawings that were published in various magazines and newspapers. Later, in college, I was fortunate enough to study with Dinnerstein at the Art Students League, and I had the opportunity to visit Burt Silverman's studio on several occasions (and once even posed for him when his scheduled model failed to show up). Now that I am older and have a better understanding of the Civil Rights movement, I'm able to appreciate the work that these two men did. In *A Sweet Smell of Roses,* I wanted to capture the simple yet powerful spirit of their work as a way of paying homage to two artists who help spread the news of an oppressed community's fight for justice and equality.

*a*fter a night of soft rain
there is a sweet smell of roses
as my sister, Minnie, and I slip
past Mama's door and out of the house
down Charlotte Street.

Past the early-morning milkman, over the cobbled bridge,
and through the curb market . . .

. . . to where everybody waits to march.

Minnie and I are only waist high to most of them.
Waist high, Minnie and me,
waist high,
holding hands
and waiting to march.

There is a sweet smell of roses
as everyone waits for Dr. King to speak.
And the colors . . .
bright light from the sun on the flowers
beside the road
as we listen to Dr. King on
the megaphone say,

Then we start to march,
Minnie and me.
We look ahead and walk faster like him.

Clapping in time with our feet.
Looking ahead,
just like him.

There is a sweet smell of roses
even as we march past the
people who scream, shout, and say,

**"You are not right.
Equality can't be yours."**

Then we look farther down the road and keep holding hands,
feeling a part of it all.
Walking our way toward freedom.

There is a sweet smell of roses as more people start marching with us, pouring out of the side streets, clapping and singing.

"Freedom!"
"Freedom!"

Then someone picks me up
and puts me on his shoulders.
Somebody picks Minnie up too,
and we are high above everybody, still marching.

There is a sweet smell of roses as
we all gather in the center of town.
All together.
All here.
Listening to Dr. King as the sun gets higher
in the sky . . .

He talks about peace,
love,
nonviolence,
and change for everybody.
And the sun gets higher in the sky. . . .

When it's time to go,
we skip back hand in hand.
Minnie and me.
Singing freedom songs along
the streets.

Through the curb market, over the cobbled bridge, and past the mailman . . .

. . . to our house on Charlotte Street.

Then there is Mama,
worried face,
waiting there for us.

She smiles after a while,
hugging us,
then takes our hands.

And as we tell her about the march,
the curtains float apart,

and there is a sweet smell of roses all through our house.